Blue
Goes to School

by Angela C. Santomero
illustrated by David B. Levy

Simon Spotlight/Nick Jr.

New York   London   Toronto   Sydney   Singapore

To Joyce, Rachel, Stacey, and Victoria. My very favorite friends from school!—A. C. S.

Dedicated to my teachers Michael Sporn, Robert Marianetti, and Howard Beckerman . . .
I will always be a pupil—D. B. L.

Note to Parents from Creators
Welcome to Blue's school! In this story, preschoolers will follow Blue through a day at school and help her figure out some tough situations. This book focuses on preschool pro-social situations and provides strategies for how to think about dealing with them. It is our desire to use Blue as a model for how a preschooler might stop, think, and act when in a tough situation. Happy reading!

Based on the TV series *Blue's Clues*® created by Traci Paige Johnson, Todd Kessler,
and Angela C. Santomero as seen on Nick Jr.®
On *Blue's Clues*, Steve is played by Steven Burns.

SIMON SPOTLIGHT
An imprint of Simon & Schuster Children's Publishing Division
1230 Avenue of the Americas
New York, New York 10020
Manufactured in the United States of America   30 29 28 27 26 25 24 23
ISBN 0-689-83280-X

Blue has a big day ahead of her. She is going to school! Blue has everything all ready. She has her backpack all packed with her smock for painting, her favorite book for reading time, and her lunch that Mr. Salt and Mrs. Pepper have made.

Blue's school is so big! Look at all of the different things Blue is going to do today at school. There's the paint corner, the block corner, and the reading rug.

"Welcome, class!" says Miss Marigold, Blue's teacher. "Everyone please put your things away in your cubbyhole and come sit down for circle time!"

But Blue's not sure which cubbyhole belongs to her. They all look so much alike! Can you help Blue find her cubbyhole?

Thanks for helping Blue find her cubbyhole! Now she can sit in circle time next to Magenta. Magenta and Blue have been friends for a long time. "Today," says Miss Marigold, "we are going to share our favorite things in circle time."

Magenta shares her paintbrushes. Orange Kitten shares her ball.
Green Puppy shares her blocks . . . that she loves to knock over.
What should Blue share?

Blue wants to share a picture of her favorite game, Blue's Clues!
'Cause that's Blue's favorite thing. "Thank you for sharing," says
Miss Marigold. "And now let's go have art time!"

What do you think Blue will paint during art time?

Look, Blue is painting a picture of her house. Magenta is painting a picture of Purple Kangaroo eating purple grapes. Oh, no! Magenta used all of the purple paint! And Blue needs the color purple to paint the door on her house! What do you think Blue should do?

Do you think Blue should just give up and stop painting? Or do you think Blue should mix two colors and make more purple paint?

Make more purple paint? It looks like Blue thinks that's a great idea!
But which two colors should Blue use to make purple? Do you know?

Good job! Blue can mix the colors red and blue to make purple.
Now Blue can finish her painting. Phew! That was a tough
situation. "Now it's time to read on the reading rug," says
Miss Marigold.

Blue loves reading time. She's even brought her favorite book, "A Puppy's Day," to school today. But, look! Green Puppy is sitting in Blue's spot on the reading rug! Blue always sits right next to Magenta! What should Blue do?

Should Blue make Green Puppy move out of her favorite spot?
Or should Blue sit somewhere else today?

Sit somewhere else? Yeah, Blue thinks that's the best idea too! As Blue looks for a new place to sit, Purple Kangaroo calls out, "Blue! Come sit over here next to me and listen to the story."

A Puppy's Day

Once upon a time, there was a little who wanted to take a nap. But she couldn't get anyone to figure out what she wanted. So she ran around the leaving clues. The left a on a blanket. The puppy left a on a . And then she left a on a . And then we figured out that it was the 's naptime! The End!

Now it's lunchtime! Blue takes out her favorite lunchbox. Inside is a picture of her Blue's Clues family! Oh, look! Blue's napkin has a note on it from . . . guess who? Uh-oh! As Blue reaches over to take a sip of her milk, she accidentally spills it all over Orange Kitten! What do you think Blue should do?

Should Blue clean up the spilled milk? Or should Blue just sit there and be sad?

Help clean up? Good idea! Blue cleans up her spilled milk and apologizes to Orange Kitten. "That's okay, Blue," says Orange Kitten. "That happened to me yesterday, remember? Here! Do you want to share some of my milk?"

"It was so nice to learn and play with you today. Don't forget to bring all of your things home with you," says Miss Marigold.

Do you remember what Blue needs to bring home? Can you help her find everything?

You found everything! Good job! Thank you for all of your help at school! You are just so smart handling those tough situations!